MR. HORROX AND THE GRATCH
BY
JAMES REEVES

PICTURES BY
QUENTIN BLAKE

WELLINGTON PUBLISHING
CHICAGO

Mr. Horrox and the Gratch

First published in 1969 by Abelard-Schuman, London

Published in the United States of America in 1991

Wellington Publishing, Inc.
P.O. Box 14877
Chicago, Illinois 60614

Library of Congress Cataloging-in-Publication Data

Reeves, James.
Mr. Horrox and the Gratch/by James Reeves;
pictures by Quentin Blake.
Summary: With the help of a spirit called the Gratch,
an artist becomes very successful by changing his
style of painting.
[1. Artists—Fiction. 2. Painting—Fiction.]
I. Blake, Quentin, ill. II. Title.
PZ7.R257Mr 1991
[E]—dc20   91-13326

ISBN 0-922984-08-5

Binding reinforced for library use

Typeset in Bookman Light by Publishers Typesetters, Inc., Chicago
Printed and bound in Singapore

Mr. Horrox painted pictures. He lived in the West Country, and his pictures were mostly of old cottages, farmyards and quaint village streets. They were very lifelike.

When they were finished, he took them to London to Mr. Smart, the art dealer. Mr. Smart hung them in his picture gallery and sold them to anyone who would buy them. In this way Mr. Horrox was able to earn a living, for his needs were simple. He liked best to sit in the sun at a street corner, smoking his pipe and painting his pictures. When he wanted a change, he went fishing.

Then one day Mr. Smart, the dealer, said to him, "You know, Horrox, my customers are beginning to get tired of farmyards and cottage doors with roses around them. Why not take a trip and see if you can find something different to paint?"

So Mr. Horrox rented a tiny cottage in Scotland, where he could paint waterfalls, Highland cattle and pine trees in the sunset.

Mrs. Brodie, a kind, neat person who lived in a cottage not far away, came and cleaned for him, made the bed and cooked his dinner.

"You'll be comfortable here," she told him as she was leaving on the evening of his first day, "only be careful of the Gratch. There's one in your cottage. He's a hundred years old or more, but he's very playful. He'll be all right if you give him plenty of string."

"What is he?" asked Mr. Horrox.

"He's sort of a wee spirit."

"What's he like, and what shall I do if I see him?"

"You'll not see him. Nobody ever has. He's invisible. He's mischievous, but he'll do you no harm provided you give him his string."

But Mr. Horrox forgot about the string, and in a day or two he forgot about the Gratch. It must be some country superstition. Such things didn't bother him. On the second day he took his painting things and went into the hills to paint Highland cattle. They were very lifelike.

Next day he went to the Lowlands and made a picture of Lowland cattle drinking from a stream. They too were lifelike.

On the fourth day Mr. Horrox made a lifelike painting of a sheepdog. After supper he smoked a pipe and went to bed.

Next morning he noticed something strange. He had left two canvases with no pictures on them leaning against the wall in the living room. On one of them there was a pattern in a thick, black line.

Mr. Horrox frowned. He told himself it must have been some naughty child who had opened the window and crept into the cottage early in the morning to play with his brushes and paints. And of course, he never thought of the Gratch.

After breakfast he once more took the other empty canvas into the glen and began a picture of a waterfall. He was pleased with it and wrote on the back "Waterfall at Glen Barra." He always wrote the names of his pictures on the back.

Next morning he was very surprised to find that this picture had been covered with a light blue paint and another picture, this time in brown and red lines, had been painted on top of it. He knew it was the picture he had been working on the day before, because on the back was written "Waterfall at Glen Barra."

"This is really too much," he said.

He was so annoyed that he did no painting that day but took his fishing rod to catch fish in the mountain stream and calm his mind.

Next morning another of his pictures had been spoiled.
It was the one of the sheepdog. It had been covered all over
with purple paint and an interesting pattern in pink and
white painted on top. But Mr. Horrox had no time to be
annoyed, because at that moment a messenger arrived from
the post office with a telegram. It said that Mr. Smart was
on his way through Scotland and would visit Mr. Horrox
that very day.

When Mr. Smart arrived, Mr. Horrox showed him the Highland cattle and the Lowland cattle. Mr. Smart shook his head.

"H'm," said the dealer, "I'm not sure that the public will like these any better than cottages with roses 'round the door. As far as London is concerned, cows are definitely out."

Then his eye fell on the line drawings standing against the wall in a corner.

"But what are these?" he asked excitedly. "By Jove, Horrox, you're on to something new!"

Mr. Horrox hardly knew what to say.

"Oh, they're just an experiment," he mumbled, turning rather red. "Nothing much really. I was—er—just amusing myself."

"But they're most *interesting*," said Mr. Smart. "I like that nervous line, and your tone values are strong. This is just what people want nowadays—*abstracts*." (People who talk about painting *always* talk this way.) "I'm glad you've given up that old realistic stuff."

He turned one of the pictures over.

"'Sheepdog on the Alert'," he read. "Yes, I see. A most original treatment. Now if you can turn out a dozen or so more like these, you can have an exhibition at my gallery in London."

Mr. Horrox promised to do his best. Before going to bed that night he wrote on the back of a new canvas "Pine Trees in the Moonlight" and left it leaning against the wall.

Next morning the canvas had been painted all over in orange with a curly pattern in pale green in the center. Mr. Horrox was delighted. At this rate there would be no difficulty in sending Mr. Smart all the abstract pictures he wanted. If this was what people liked in London, they could have it. Suddenly Mr. Horrox remembered the Gratch—the invisible wee spirit that Mrs. Brodie had told him about.

"Perhaps it is the Gratch who is painting all the pictures," Mr. Horrox said to himself. "What can you expect from a Gratch but pictures like that?"

He was so pleased to think that the Gratch was doing all his work for him that once more he decided to spend the day fishing. In the evening he was so tired that he completely forgot to leave out a canvas. Nor did he put his fishing rod away; he just stood it up in a corner.

In the morning he was dismayed to find that there was no picture but only a tangle of fishing line on the floor. Mr. Horrox untangled the line and wound it up on the reel.

"Oh well," he thought, "if the little fellow is going to do no more pictures, I'd better start painting some myself. Meanwhile, I'll send this stuff to Smart."

So he went to the village for some brown paper and a big ball of string. But he did not forget to leave out a new canvas at night before going to bed.

Next day he found the canvas out on the floor untouched, but with an interesting pattern of string spread out upon it. He tidied up the string and began to paint, using the canvas he had left out the night before.

He did not find it very hard to paint like the Gratch. All he had to do was to choose some exciting color, like lemon yellow or rich purply blue, cover the canvas with it, and paint lines on it in some other striking color. Then he would write on the back "Harvest at Glen Barra" or "Storm over the Loch."

Every day he did this, and every night the Gratch came and played with the string and left Mr. Horrox's pictures alone. As long as the Gratch had plenty of string to play with, he wasn't interested in paints and brushes.

Sometimes Mr. Horrox would copy the string patterns left by the Gratch; sometimes he would make up patterns of his own. Soon he became even better that the invisible wee spirit.

By the end of the month there was a really surprising collection of modern pictures, mostly the work of Mr. Horrox himself.

He took the pictures to London, where Mr. Smart hung them in his gallery.

They caused great excitement in the art world, and a lot of people bought them.

So once more Mr. Horrox was able to earn enough money to live comfortably and go fishing without worrying about the future.

As for the Gratch, he stayed in the tiny cottage in Scotland, mischievous and invisible, playing happily with the ball of string left by Mr. Horrox.